IN A

DYSTOPIA?

An Interactive Doomsday Adventure

by ANTHONY WACHOLTZ

illustrated by JAMES NATHAN

raintree

a Capstone company — publishers for children

Raintree is an imprint of Capstone Global Library Limited, a company incorporated in England and Wales having its registered office at 7 Pilgrim Street, London, EC4V 6LB – Registered company number: 6695582

www.raintree.co.uk
myorders@raintree.co.uk

Editorial Credits
Mari Bolte, editor; Bobbie Nuytten, designer; Jo Miller, media researcher; Gene Bentdahl, production specialist; Nathan Gassman, creative director

ISBN 978 1 4747 1105 0
20 19 18 17 16
10 9 8 7 6 5 4 3 2 1

British Library Cataloguing in Publication Data
A full catalogue record for this book is available from the British Library.

Photo Credits
Shutterstock: Andrew Burgess, (background, throughout), Melkor3D, 104, photka, 107, WELBURNSTUART, 102

Every effort has been made to contact copyright holders of material reproduced in this book. Any omissions will be rectified in subsequent printings if notice is given to the publisher.

All the internet addresses (URLs) given in this book were valid at the time of going to press. However, due to the dynamic nature of the internet, some addresses may have changed,or sites may have changed or ceased to exist since publication. While the author and publisher regret any inconvenience this may cause readers, no responsibility for any such changes can be accepted by either the author or the publisher.

Printed in China.

CONTENTS

ABOUT YOUR
ADVENTURE

You are living through a dark and dangerous time. It's a bleak and desolate dystopian world where only pockets of humanity remain. Will you be one of the few who survive? Start off by turning the page. Then follow the directions at the bottom of each page. The choices you make will change the outcome. After you finish one path, go back and read the others to see how the decisions you make change your fate. Do you have what it takes to survive life after doomsday?

YOU CHOOSE the path you take through a dystopian future.

SURVIVING THE END OF THE WORLD

THWIP!

Your arrow whizzes through the air before striking a tree. Pinned to the tree is a large squirrel – the first animal you've caught in weeks. You pull on the arrow, but it's gone too far into the wood. Snapping the arrow in disgust, you pull the squirrel off and put it in your rucksack. You'll be able to add meat to your tin of beans tonight, but now you're down to your last two arrows.

You walk through the woods, checking the traps you set earlier in the week. You can't believe your luck – two of the traps contain rabbits!

The sun is starting to set, so you decide to call it a day. After walking for a kilometre or so, keeping the sun at your back, you push aside some heavy brush and step through to find your cabin.

Turn the page.

A smile spreads across your face. Although you've only been staying at the cabin for two weeks, it's the first time you've felt at home in a long, long time. After travelling more than 50 kilometres over six days, scavenging and looking for shelter, you couldn't have asked for a better place.

You walk up to the front door, but before you grab the door handle, you hear muffled voices from inside the cabin. You ease around the side of the cabin as the front door swings open. You peek around the corner to see three rugged-looking men emerge.

A tall man with black hair and a goatee saunters off the porch, a long-handled axe slung over his shoulder. Another man with a leather jacket eyes the trees warily, his right hand resting on the pistol sticking out of his jeans. The third one, a short middle-aged man with broad shoulders, struggles to carry two over-stuffed sacks.

"You made the right call once again, Raven," says the tall man.

"What a find!" the short man exclaims, digging his head into one of the sacks. "This is the biggest haul we've come 'cross since that group we robbed last month."

"You can look at the loot later, Bulldog!" says Raven, smacking him on the back of the head. "Let's get moving. Wolf, grab one of these sacks before Bulldog hurts himself."

The couple you ran into a few weeks ago told you about a ruthless group of thieves with animal nicknames. They call themselves the Stalkers. They steal food, supplies – anything they want. You shudder, remembering the stories of the methods they use to collect things.

Turn the page.

Your first instinct is to stay hidden until they leave, but the rumble in your stomach makes you think twice. They're walking off with all the tinned food you've scavenged over the last month. Apart from the squirrel and two rabbits in your rucksack, you've got nothing else to eat.

But what good is food if you're not alive to eat it? You have a bow and two arrows, while they have an axe and a gun – and they're much bigger than you. There's no way you can take them on now, but maybe you could follow them and steal back the food when their guard is down.

To follow the Stalkers, go to page 11.
To stay hidden until the Stalkers leave, turn to page 44.

You're not willing to give up on your food stash. Over the years since the pandemic wiped out most of the world's population, you've learned to move without being seen. If you stay behind the trees, you might be able to follow them without them knowing.

After about a kilometre, you're no longer worried about being heard by the Stalkers. Bulldog has talked the entire time.

"I'm telling ya, the monster scared me to death. That Echo was twice my size," he says. "I could barely see it in the dark."

"Will you just be quiet?" sneers Wolf, eyeing the path ahead watchfully. "I can't hear anything lurking in the woods with all your yammering."

The Stalkers continue on in silence, and you're left wondering about the creature Bulldog was talking about. Surviving in this post-apocalyptic world is hard enough – you don't need any other dangers to deal with.

Turn the page.

As darkness descends over the forest, the Stalkers walk through a small grove of trees to a secluded house. Raven enters first, followed by Bulldog and Wolf. You hunch over and scurry to the side of the house. You don't relish the thought of staying outside in the dark, but you'd probably get caught if you tried to enter the house now.

You tuck yourself into the corner between the porch and the house to block the cool night wind. The exhaustion from your long day sets in, and you pass out with your head resting awkwardly against the wall of the house.

SNAP!

You jolt awake at the sound of a branch cracking. Your heart pounds, but you try to hold your breath, straining your ears for another sound. Within seconds, another branch breaks, then another. Whatever is moving in the brush is getting closer.

You stand up and ease your way to the porch, trying not to make any sudden movements. You walk up the steps backwards as you scan the trees for movement. As you reach the top step, you see two small glints of light amongst the trees ahead. With a shudder, you realize the lights are the reflection of two beady eyes – eyes that are staring right at you.

The creature emerges from the trees, its head low. Although it's hard to see in detail, you can tell the sleek beast walks on four legs. From its spiny head to its long, slender tail, its scaly skin shimmers in the pale moonlight.

The beast advances slowly, its bright eyes gleaming through the darkness. You jump nervously as your back hits the front door with a thud. As the creature rears back to pounce, the door clicks open, and a hand grabs your coat. Wolf pulls you inside, slams the door and drags you to the basement cellar, closing the door down over your heads.

Turn the page.

"Why did you save me?" you ask.

A shrill shriek from outside makes Wolf pause before responding. "Raven has other plans for you," he says, his eyes on the cellar door.

"Indeed I do," says Raven, stepping out of the shadows. "But we're not cruel men. We'll let you pick your fate. A group of survivors are living in the nearby city. They have masses of food and supplies, but they also carry weapons and ammunition. You can infiltrate their group and help us 'borrow' some of their goods."

"What's my other choice?"

"Although Echoes hunt in packs, they are territorial creatures. One whiff of a fellow Echo, and the others scatter. That's why it pays to have an Echo near by. And because those things shriek like banshees to communicate, it's safer to have a dead one. You'll be our bait, and if you survive, we may even let you go."

To infiltrate the survivor group, turn to page 16.
To act as bait for an Echo, turn to page 21.

"Not much of a choice. I'd never survive as Echo bait," you say.

"Then get some sleep," Raven replies. "You've got a big day tomorrow."

Wolf throws a wet, mouldy pillow at you. "Sweet dreams, kid," he says as he grabs a shotgun from the corner. "C'mon, guys – the Echo's shriek will have signalled others. If we fire a few warning shots, they won't risk trying to enter the house."

They climb the stairs with Raven exiting the crawl space last. He smirks at you as he drops the wooden door with a slam, and the room goes pitch black. You throw the pillow aside and wonder how you're actually going to sleep. There's no point in trying to search for a way out. With your luck, you'd stumble in the dark and cut yourself. Instead, you curl up on the hard floor and think about what might happen when the Stalkers return.

"Rise and shine, kid! You've got work to do!"

Light floods into the cellar. You squint your eyes as a shadowy figure descends the steps. It grabs your arm and pulls you to your feet. You stumble up the steps, your eyes still half shut.

"All right, here's what you're going to do," Raven says, sitting in a brown one-armed recliner. "We're going to give you some of your food back. But don't get too excited – you don't get to eat it."

Bulldog chuckles behind you. You turn just in time to catch a tin of vegetables.

"I'll give you precise directions on how to reach the house," Wolf says, clamping a hand on your shoulder. "Your job will be to gain the trust of everyone inside. Then you'll let us in after they go to sleep."

Turn the page.

"And don't try to run," says Bulldog as he nods his head towards a sniper rifle. "Wolf's a dead shot."

"Then why doesn't he just take out everyone in the house from a distance?" you ask, shrugging free of Wolf's grasp.

"Kid, you don't make it this long by being reckless," says Raven. "Even if he was able to get the first few, the ones left could return fire or lock the place down. That makes it more difficult for us. With my plan, we won't give them a chance to react. And if you tip them off about us, you'll be the first to die."

"Time's a-tickin', kiddo," says Wolf. "Trust is hard to come by after dark."

Bulldog thrusts one of the sacks of food into your hands. Raven pulls out a map and gives you a detailed route to reach the house. With one final shove, you're out of the door and on your way.

Turn the page.

Sweat pours down your neck and back. You've been walking an hour in the hot sun with the sack of food slung over your shoulder. Just as your feet begin to throb, you see the target house. You cross the street, let out a nervous sigh, and trudge up the steps. Before you can knock, the front door cracks open.

"What do you want?" a woman demands.

"I'm just looking for shelter," you say, your voice quivering. "Please let me in."

"How did you know we were here?"

"I was trying to avoid a pack of Echoes last night when I saw someone enter the house," you say, reciting the words Raven gave you earlier. "I waited to come back during the day so you wouldn't be startled."

The person behind the door goes quiet, probably mulling over your story. In the silence, your conscience nags at you. Should you continue the act, or should you try to warn the people who live here?

To stick to the Stalkers' plan, turn to page 25.
To warn the person about the Stalkers, turn to page 26.

"Do what you want with me," you say. "But I'm not going to endanger other people's lives."

Raven chuckles. "It amazes me you've stayed alive this long with any morals."

"Raven, we should act now," Wolf says. "The Echo has signalled others. If we move quickly, we can take it down and deter other Echoes from getting close."

"You're right," says Raven. "Lucky for you, kid, we already have everything set up. We're going to send you out the back door. If you don't want to be eaten, hook yourself to the pulley system."

Raven guides you to the kitchen window and points to the backyard. A series of pulleys extend from the house and ends with a single rope with a hook.

"When the Echo gets close," he says, "Bulldog will haul you up out of reach. Then Wolf and I will subdue the beast."

Turn the page.

Bulldog steps towards you, holding out a makeshift harness. "You best get the hook in the slot real fast, or we're gonna have to find new bait." His wide grin displays a set of crooked and decaying teeth.

"Thanks for the advice," you mutter as you step into the harness. Bulldog roughly adjusts a few of the cords until you're snug in the tethers. Then he backs off as Raven steps up to give you directions.

"We need you to make some noise to attract the Echo," Raven says. "These things have incredibly acute hearing, so it needs to come from you if this is going to work. Don't get any clever ideas about clamming up, or you and I are going to have a problem later." He pulls a jagged machete from a sheath attached to his calf and waves it in front of you.

Turn the page.

"Let's get it over with," you say with as much courage as you can muster.

Raven stares at you for a moment, then chuckles. "You heard the kid. Let's move."

Raven and Wolf cross to the opposite side of the house, guns at the ready. Bulldog rests his hand on the back door and gives you a questioning look. You nod, and he flings the door open. You run to the hook and attach it to your harness. Bulldog slips around the corner of the house and pulls the rope. You let out a grunt as the pulley lifts you off the ground. The rope spins slowly, and you see Bulldog's face peeking around the corner. He raises his eyebrows at you expectantly.

To make noise, turn to page 36.
To stay quiet, turn to page 38.

"Where did you come from?" asks the voice behind the door.

"I travelled here from Chanhaster," you respond. "I've been staying in the woods, but the Echoes found my camp last night."

"Sorry, kiddo, but we've got enough people to care for already. It's best if you keep moving."

"If you don't let me in the house, they'll kill me!" you blurt out, desperate.

Someone inside the house gasps. "You were going to help them rob us, weren't you? Get out of here!"

A gunshot rings out as a bullet splinters the wood in the door frame 10 centimetres from your head. The door slams shut as a second shot echoes through the air. A sharp pain stings your neck, and you slump onto the porch. You wonder if Wolf missed his mark or if the Stalkers had no further use for you. It doesn't really matter now as a black haze clouds your eyes.

THE END

To follow another path, turn to page 10.
To learn more about dystopias, turn to page 103.

"Listen carefully," you whisper. "I've got a rifle aimed at my head. They want me to gain your trust so I can help them rob you. Unless you let me inside right now, they'll kill me, I'm sure of it."

More silence. Then the door opens a little. You step through the doorway to find a dozen sets of eyes trained on you. The woman who talked to you shuts the door quickly.

"You're safe. For now," she says. "My name's Andi. What exactly is going on?"

You swallow hard, both relieved to be out of eyeshot of the Stalkers and nervous to be the centre of attention. "The Stalkers gave me… "

"The Stalkers? You led the Stalkers here?" a man in the back cries.

"The Stalkers already knew you were here," you say sullenly. "They gave me a choice: Gain your trust and help them steal your supplies or be bait for an Echo. If I didn't do what they said, I'd be dead right now."

Turn the page.

"Great, just great," the man mumbles. "I wish you'd picked Echo bait, kid. Now we're all dead."

"Take it easy, Jason," Andi scolds. "You would have done the same thing. Anyways, what's done is done. Now we have to decide what to do next."

"I say we go on the offensive," says Jason. "Show them they can't mess with us. Let's fire a few rounds off and they'll take the hint."

"Are you serious?" asks Andi. "Do you want them to kill us?"

"Would you rather they think we're weak? They know where we live. They'll have eyes on us at all times." Some of the others murmur in agreement.

"As far as the Stalkers know, their plan is still in effect," replies Andi. "That gives us the element of surprise. As long as our new friend goes along with it, we can set a trap."

To go on the offensive, go to page 29.
To lure the Stalkers into a trap, turn to page 32.

"The Stalkers wanted to send me in first because they're afraid of your fire-power," you say. "If you show them you mean business, they might back off."

"The kid's got the right idea," Jason smirks. "I'll fire a few shots from the upstairs window."

"They've got a sniper rifle, Jason!" cries Andi. "They'll see you!"

Jason scoffs and tromps up the stairs with an assault rifle hanging at his side. The other people in the house look at each other nervously while a few look up at the creaking floor above them. You hear the window upstairs click open, followed by the boom of six shots fired.

"The kid's with us now!" shouts Jason. "You best move on if—"

Jason's words are cut off as a shot rings out in the distance. A thud overhead sends Andi racing to the stairwell.

Turn the page.

You follow Andi up the stairs and find Jason on the floor with a hand on his throat. You drop to your knees next to him just as his hand falls from his neck. He's gone.

You jump as gunfire erupts downstairs. Andi is frozen in fear, so you grab her arm and pull her into the wardrobe. Two muffled voices travel up the stairs and head directly to the room you're in. Andi squeezes your hand as you hear someone walk to the window and pick up the assault rifle.

"You think the kid ran off?"

The voice belongs to Bulldog. You shudder when Raven replies, "No, the kid's not far… "

The wardrobe door swings open to reveal Raven's snarling face. He levels his gun at you and says, "This is a world of second chances, kid. You don't get a third."

"Sorry, Andi," you whimper, as Bulldog walks to the wardrobe and aims his shotgun.

THE END

To follow another path, turn to page 10.
To learn more about dystopias, turn to page 103.

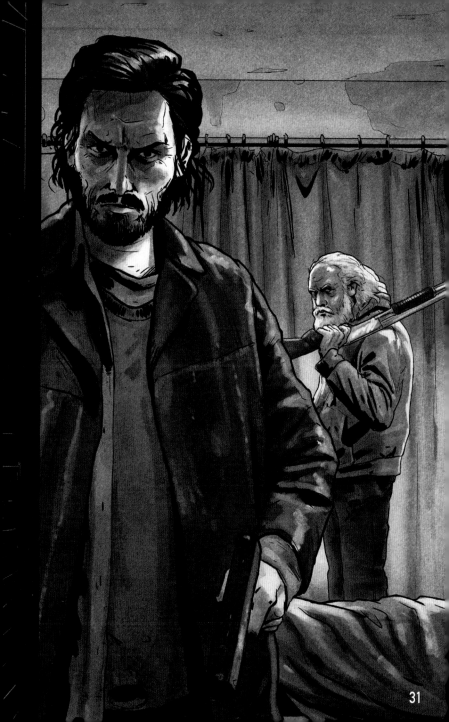

"Andi's right," you say. "These guys are ruthless, and they won't be scared off by a few gunshots. They'll be in the backyard next door by nightfall. The plan was to wait until everyone fell asleep. Then I would let them in through the back door."

"They're going to be armed to the teeth," says Jason snidely. "Even if we catch them off guard, how do we disarm them?"

"They're only coming for the supplies," you say. "Their leader flat-out said they didn't want to take on your entire group, even in an ambush. Once I load their arms up with supplies, they won't have time to reach for their guns once you spring into action."

Jason opens his mouth, then shuts it. He raises his eyebrows and nods. "All right then. Sounds like we have a plan."

Andi organizes the group and gives each person a place to hide when the Stalkers enter the house. As night falls, Andi approaches you. "Good luck. And be safe. You're risking a lot to help us." She pats you on the shoulder, then retreats to a small space behind the stairs.

You let out a big sigh before going through the back door. You slide along the fencing separating the two houses and almost let out a yelp when a hand grabs your arm.

"You ready, kid?" asks Wolf. You nod, and the three Stalkers follow you back to the house. You can feel Wolf staring at you, and it makes the hair on the back of your neck prickle. You lead them to the room with the supplies, and Bulldog and Wolf start to stack items in their arms. Raven pulls a pistol out from his waistband and eyes the rest of the house. Your heart races. *What should I do?*

Turn the page.

When Bulldog and Wolf finish loading up, the Stalkers move towards the back door.

"NOW!" Andi screams. Bulldog and Wolf freeze in surprise, but Raven immediately swings his pistol around. Without thinking, you race towards him and lower your shoulder. The gun fires. A stinging pain shoots through your leg. You collapse but knock Raven to the ground in the process. Andi's friends swarm the Stalkers and overpower them.

"Are you OK?" asks Andi, kneeling next to you. "Jacqueline! Get over here!"

A woman runs over and rolls up the leg of your jeans. "The shot just grazed the calf." She looks at you and smiles. "You're going to be fine."

Andi helps you lay back gently as Jacqueline wraps a bandage around the wound. After tying up the Stalkers, the others take turns thanking you. You've certainly earned a place in their group.

THE END
To follow another path, turn to page 10.
To learn more about dystopias, turn to page 103.

"Over here," you shout as you spin at the end of the rope. "Um – food on a rope, come and get it!"

The only sound is the wind gently moving through the trees. When you spin and face Bulldog, he furrows his brow and nods at you.

"I'm – uh – hanging out here, waiting for an Echo!" You know you sound ridiculous, but you don't know what else to say. As you rotate away from the house, you see a pair of eyes shining at you from across the yard. It's an Echo! It walks towards you, curiosity on its face.

"There it is! Hoist me up!" you shout. But nothing happens except your continued spinning. You struggle, which only makes you spin faster. The Echo lowers its head and advances. "Hey! Bulldog! Pull the rope now!"

The black creature moves within two body lengths of you. It sits back on its haunches, ready to pounce.

He'll pull me up any second now, you think, trying to convince yourself you'll be safe. But as the Echo launches in the air, you realize the Stalkers had no intention of you surviving. The Echo's claws pierce your right shoulder, and the rope immediately snaps. You grunt in pain as you hit the ground hard, the Echo's full weight on top of you. Without hesitation, the beast sinks its teeth into your neck, causing a wave of intense pain that seems to shoot through your entire body.

A series of gunshots explode in the air. The Echo cries out briefly before tipping over lifelessly on its side. You press your hand against your neck to stop the flow of blood, but your eyelids are too heavy. Your vision starts to fade, but in that last moment you see Raven. "You did great, kid," he says with a chuckle. "Best bait we ever had."

THE END
To follow another path, turn to page 10.
To learn more about dystopias, turn to page 103.

You stare Bulldog down, one eyebrow raised in defiance. You purse your lips tightly, refusing to talk.

Bulldog's face bunches up in anger. He yanks the rope several times, causing you to bob up and down and spin wildly, but you still keep quiet.

"Make some noise!" he says through gritted teeth.

Expecting silence, you instead hear a growl from across the yard. The Echo emerges from the shadows and slinks towards Bulldog, who screams and releases the rope. You land hard on your knees but are able to stay upright.

Bulldog reaches for his pistol, but the Echo is quicker. He launches at the Stalker, knocking him backwards and out of sight around the house. Bloodcurdling screams pierce the night air.

You fumble with the clasp before slipping out of the harness. Your plan worked, but you're not sure what to do next.

To go back into the house, turn to page 40.
To run for the woods, turn to page 42.

You remember Raven saying that Echoes hunt in packs. If that's true, there may be more of the creatures near by. As much as you don't want to go back into the Stalkers' house, it's the safest option you have.

You open the back door, cringing as the rusty hinges squeak. You slide through the opening and shut the door as quietly as you can.

You go from room to room, looking for something to defend yourself. You come up empty but notice a map on the kitchen worktop. One of the blocks in the nearby town has a note scribbled next to it:

BRICK HOUSE ON BOULDER AVENUE. AT LEAST 8 SURVIVORS. LOTS OF LOOT.

That must be the group of survivors Raven was talking about. You grab the map from the worktop and settle in a dark corner to study it by moonlight. Hours pass, and the light of the rising sun starts to peek through the windows.

You don't plan to stick around to find out what happened to Raven and Wolf. You exit through the back door and run for the trees. Then you run along the map route, now etched in your memory. Before long you reach the house on Boulder Avenue.

A voice stops you dead in your tracks.

"Wolf and Bulldog are dead because of you!"

You spin around to see Raven charging at you with an axe. Before you can react, a gunshot stops Raven in his advance.

"Drop the axe!" a woman shouts from beside the brick house. Two others emerge behind her. The woman walks over to you as the others advance on Raven. "We'll take care of him," she says. "Go up to the house and tell them Andi said you could stay with us."

You smile, allowing yourself to hope for the first time in as long as you can remember.

THE END

To follow another path, turn to page 10.
To learn more about dystopias, turn to page 103.

You sprint for the trees, adrenaline racing through your veins after the close encounter.

I hope I can find another house in the dark, you think. *I might be able to…*

A growling noise coming from your right interrupts your thoughts. You can barely make out the silhouette of an Echo striding by your side less than ten metres away. You whip your head around as another growl eases out of the darkness to your left.

You retreat a few steps before you turn and make a break for the Stalkers' house. Before you can take five steps, one of the creatures rams you with its head and knocks you down. You try to scramble to your feet, but a searing pain tears through your left leg as the other Echo swipes at you with its clawed paw. You cower in the foetal position as the two Echoes close in, licking their chops.

THE END

To follow another path, turn to page 10.
To learn more about dystopias, turn to page 103.

You're cross that the Stalkers took your entire food stash, but you won't let anger cloud your judgment. You wait until the three men disappear into the trees before setting off in the opposite direction.

As you reach the edge of the forest near the south east part of town, your stomach starts to growl. If you're going to make a fire to cook your meal, you should do it now. You don't want to draw attention by creating flames in the dark.

You start to gather branches and tinder for the fire when a scream makes you jump. You ease quietly to the edge of the woods as a second, louder scream fills the air. Two blocks down, you can see a tough-looking man standing over a young woman. He has a firm grasp on the back of her shirt. A rusty shopping trolley full of supplies sits next to them.

To sneak up and subdue the man, turn to page 46.
To try talking to the man, turn to page 87.

The man has his back to you. If you're quiet, you could get the upper hand and help the woman subdue him. Staying on the balls of your feet, you creep towards the man as he draws a large knife out of a sheath on his belt. The woman's scream is cut short when she sees you. The man follows her gaze and swings around just as you're about to grab him. He lets go of the woman and grabs your shirt.

"What do you think you're doing, you little brat?" he says, drawing the knife to your neck. With the man's attention on you, the woman makes her escape, leaving the trolley behind. *Thanks a lot,* you think bitterly. *This is what I get for trying to help someone.*

The man pushes you towards the trolley. "Well, as you're such a brave kid, you can come back to my place and meet my pet. Then we'll see how brave you are. Now push."

You look down at the trolley, then back to the man. As if reading your thoughts, the man says, "Don't try to run. I've been living in this area for two years. There's nowhere you can go where I won't find you. And even if you can escape me, you'll just end up as lunch for an Echo."

"An Echo?" you ask as you start to push the trolley.

The man gives you a look of disbelief. "How have you survived this long and never heard of an Echo? Those creatures are crawling all over the place once the sun goes down."

The hair rises on the back of your neck. "Creatures? What kind of creatures?"

A disturbing smile creeps onto the man's face. "The government spent billions creating animal hybrids at a facility not far from here. Most of the new species didn't survive past the first generation. But the Echoes survived all too well. They became aggressive, eventually attacking the researchers and escaping from the compound."

Turn the page.

The man pauses to check a tin on the ground. When you don't say anything, he throws the tin to one side and continues. "Everyone knows that the B193 virus is what led to this barren dystopia we call Earth. But most people don't know where the Echoes came from. When the virus had spread across the globe, the government had its hands full. It was too busy trying to find an antidote to the pandemic. All the other resources were used setting up quarantine zones and organizing military groups. They couldn't afford the money or manpower needed to track down the Echoes."

"How do you know all this?" you ask. "And why are the creatures called Echoes?"

"A few months ago, I was with a group led by a top-level military agent. I suppose he realized that with the human species hanging by a thread, there was no reason to be discreet anymore. He was the one that called them Echoes. He gave them the name because of the way they communicate – through loud shrieks."

You remember hearing a shrill cry in the middle of the night a few weeks ago. Then, you had no idea what it was. Now, you're not sure you wanted to find out.

"Nothing to say? Not so tough now, are ya?" the man says with a chuckle. You continue walking in silence as the sun dips towards the horizon.

"Ah, home sweet home," the man says as you approach a large two-story house at the end of a cul-de-sac. "C'mon in. Someone will be excited to meet you."

The man's grin makes you feel uneasy. With only a few metres between you and the front door, your chance to escape is almost over. It might be all over once the door shuts.

To make a run for it, turn to page 50.
To follow the man into the house, turn to page 52.

You take a step around the trolley towards the house, looking up at the first floor. "This place is huge. Can't be all that bad."

You turn to look at the man who has walked up behind the trolley. "It's a nice place indeed," he says. "It's too bad you won't get to enjoy it for long."

As the last word leaves the man's mouth, you push the trolley into him with all your strength. The impact knocks the man over, and the trolley flips onto him as tinned food flies in all directions. This is your chance!

You sprint through the yard next to the man's house, ducking under a child's swing and cutting through a hedge.

SNAP! You cry out as a bear trap bites into your leg. Tears flow down your cheeks as you grab the metal teeth and try to pull them apart.

"You shouldn't have run," says the man. "I might have let you live a little longer."

He emerges from the hedges holding a long metal pole that ends in a thick collar. The device is fashioned tightly around the neck of a bizarre creature with features of both a panther and some sort of reptile. The creature's soft growl is somehow fierce through the muzzle wrapped around its mouth. It creeps towards you low to the ground, sniffing your snared leg while keeping its yellow-tinted eyes on you.

The man reaches out towards the creature, but a woman steps out of the shadows to stop him. "You can't take his muzzle off – he'll signal other Echoes."

"Relax," he says, undoing a buckle. "It'll be quick. It hasn't eaten in almost a week. We'll have the muzzle back on before it can call for help."

You kick at the creature with your good leg as it approaches, but you're no match for the vile beast.

THE END
To follow another path, turn to page 10.
To learn more about dystopias, turn to page 103.

What the man said about the Echo has given you second thoughts about escaping now. Maybe it would be better to wait for morning.

"Vicki!" yells the man. "Get out here and help haul in this food!" After a few moments, a young woman opens the front door. She looks at you with disgust.

"Who's this, Jake? I told you I don't want to share our rations with anyone else."

"Our pet has to eat," Jake says as he clasps his hand around your wrist. "Let's go inside, shall we?" Vicki cackles as she grabs your other wrist and forces you through the doorway.

With a push from Jake, you fall roughly into the house. You barely have time to thrust your hands down to stop you falling flat on the floor. You arch your head back and come face-to-face with a terrifying creature with black, scaly skin and thorns on its head. Drool oozes through the muzzle secured around its mouth.

But its eyes are what frighten you most. Their yellowish tint seems to glow in the shadows cast from the pale light shining through the window. The pupils are dark and oval-shaped, running vertically across each eye.

You push off from the ground and scoot backwards until your back slams against the wall. The man and woman wheeze with laughter at your reaction.

"Th-that's an E-echo?" you stammer.

"Beautiful, ain't it?" says Jake. "Specifically, that's *my* Echo. These things are wild, but after a few thwacks with a tree branch, this one has learnt its place."

The long strips of raw, open flesh on the Echo's back and arms confirm Jake's story. The creature's legs are secured with metal chains. The Echo looks at you but constantly shifts its eyes towards its captor. With a quick step forward, Jake advances towards the Echo threateningly. The Echo frantically withdraws to the corner, a frustrated growl coming from its throat.

Turn the page.

"Enough already," says Vicki. "Let's get this food inside." The two captors ease the shopping trolley through the door and into the kitchen. When they are out of sight, the Echo steps towards you again.

The Echo sniffs at you, slowly at first, then quickly moving up and down your body. It seems more curious than hungry, at least at the moment. You can't help but feel bad for it, seeing it tied up with harsh wounds all over its body.

Looking more closely at the muzzle, you see there is only a single pin locking the two pieces in place. The clasps around the Echo's wrists and ankles are simple too. Like a wristwatch, each clasp can be released by snapping apart the locked piece.

You stretch your hand slowly towards the Echo. It recoils immediately, growling fiercely.

"Settle down in there!" yells Jake from the kitchen. "You'll have your meal soon enough!"

To try removing the Echo's muzzle, turn to page 56.
To move quietly to the front door, turn to page 60.

Checking the kitchen doorway one more time, you slowly crawl on your hands and knees towards the Echo. It growls softly at first, but then it goes quiet, looking at you with curiosity. You stick your hand out towards the Echo's face, leaving it there to let it get accustomed to you. It sniffs your hand, then your arm. After staring into your eyes for a few seconds, it lies down.

You reach for the clasp holding one of its legs, but the Echo immediately jerks its head up so that the muzzle is less than an five centimetres from your hand. You pause briefly, then release the clasp as quietly as you can. The Echo pulls its leg free before looking at you eagerly to continue. Feeling comfortable to move quickly around the creature, you undo the other clasps in less than a minute. Finally, you raise both hands to slip off the muzzle.

The Echo shakes itself and arches its back, stretching its front legs. It walks over to you and bares its teeth. Before you can run, it licks the palm of your hand. You sigh with relief and extend your hand to pet the creature, being careful to avoid the wounds on its back.

"What are you *doing*?" cries Jake. He stands in the kitchen doorway, disbelief on his face. He takes one step towards you, but the Echo snarls and steps between the two of you. Jake immediately retreats into the kitchen, tripping over his own feet and slamming into the hardwood floor. The Echo pounces on him, pinning him to the ground. Jake screeches in pain as the creature's teeth pierce the flesh on his right arm. His calls alert Vicki, but she is frozen in fear at the other side of the room. You turn away from the kitchen, unsure that your stomach can handle the sickening sight.

Turn the page.

You wait a couple of minutes before walking to the kitchen. You try to prepare yourself, but you instantly gag at the sight of the grisly scene. The Echo is circling what's left of Jake and the growing dark red stain on the hardwood floor. Vicki is nowhere to be seen.

You walk back to the living room and open the front door. You pause, not knowing where to go next. You're certain you don't want to stay here, though.

The Echo walks up to you, pressing its smooth but scaly skin against your leg. It walks out the door and cranes its neck around to look at you again. Then it runs down the street, quickly disappearing into the black night.

You feel both disappointed and somewhat relieved to see the Echo go. The creature seemed friendly, but it survived brutal experimentation at the hands of humans. You could never be certain that it wouldn't turn on you without warning.

"Hey! Are you OK?"

You swivel your head in the direction of the voice and squint into the darkness. A vague shape forms out of the shadows of the house next door.

"It's me, Andi! The woman you saved from that horrible man. I'm sorry I ran off, but I didn't think we stood much of a chance alone. I knew where he lived, so I came back with help." She looks past you to the open doorway. "Where is he?"

"He's dead, no thanks to you," you say as you push past Andi. "I almost died!"

"I'm so sorry," she says. "I'll make it up to you, I promise. Come back with us. We have food, and you can get a good night's sleep while we stand guard."

To go with Andi, turn to page 65.
To reject her offer, turn to page 68.

You look at the Echo one more time before shifting your eyes to the kitchen doorway. You flatten the palms of your hands against the wall and rise slowly. As you make your way slowly to the front door, the Echo quietly whimpers. It probably wants to leave just as much as you do, but you don't have time to undo its restraints.

Your fingertips barely touch the doorknob when the Echo's whimpers turn to loud growls. Immediately, Jake stomps out of the kitchen. His eyes go wide when he sees you at the front door.

"I just can't trust you, can I?" he snarls. "Guess we'll have to put you in the cage."

Jake grabs you by the shoulder and throws you roughly to the floor. Before you can get away, he binds your legs together by wrapping duct tape around your ankles. He rolls you onto your stomach as Vicki puts a knee into your back. Cringing in pain, you can feel Jake apply the duct tape around your wrists as well.

Jake hooks his arms under yours and drags you down the basement steps. The air reeks of mould and dust. Then you see the "cage" – a dog kennel big enough for a German Shepherd. Jake opens the door and slides you through the opening, locking the door in place with a padlock. You immediately kick at one of the walls, but the kennel doesn't move. That's when you notice the corners have been welded solidly together, and the bottom ridge has been welded to the floor.

"Sleep tight!" Jake says with a chuckle. "It might not be too comfortable, but don't worry. You'll only be in there for a couple hours. My Echo needs to eat, ya know." He winks at you, but you just glare back at him.

Turn the page.

He climbs the basement stairs and slams the door, leaving the room in darkness. Fading sunlight shines through the only window not completely covered with towels. Muffled voices filter through the ceiling, but you can't make out what's being said. After a few minutes, you hear chains dragging against the floor above you. The front door slams, then nothing but silence – not even growls or whimpers from the Echo.

Without enough room to stretch out, the best you can do is lay with your head down and your knees tucked into your chest. The exhaustion from the day hits you, and you fall asleep.

You wake up in complete darkness. How much time has passed? No light is coming through the window, so you must have slept for at least a couple of hours. You shout for help, even though you don't expect a response.

Turn the page.

You doubt you can break free, but you have to try. You work your wrists back and forth to loosen the duct tape. It's a slow process, but eventually you pull free from the sticky bond. You remove the tape from around your ankles and try kicking at the kennel wall again. You reach through the bars and pull down on the padlock with both hands. Nothing works.

As you scan the room for anything that might help, your eyes land on a dull light coming through the partially covered window. You wonder if something happened to Jake and Vicki – they've been gone a lot longer than a couple of hours.

When another day passes, you realize no one is coming back for you. Your stomach groans, and your back hurts from being in the kennel. You shout out for help, but your voice cracks from dehydration. You can only muster a tiny hope that someone will stumble across you while searching for supplies.

THE END

To follow another path, turn to page 10.
To learn more about dystopias, turn to page 103.

You're cross with Andi, but you can't pass up the opportunity. You follow her, unable to see more than a few metres in the pitch dark. You almost run into her when she stops between two houses.

"Let me go first." she says. "Wait here."

She strides through the grass and raps on the back door of a brick house. The door opens a crack, and she begins talking to an unseen person. After a minute, she waves you over. As soon as you enter the house, a man steps up to you with his arms crossed.

"Andi, we have to be more careful about who we let into our house," he says sternly. "Ramon's group have already brought someone back tonight – a crazy woman. No offence, kid, but we can't take in more people than we can provide for."

"Jason, I was ambushed," says Andi. "This boy stepped in so I could escape. Like a coward, I ran. Bringing him here was the only way I could make things right." Jason sighs but nods in agreement.

Turn the page.

Crazy woman? Could he be talking about Vicki? you wonder. Your question is answered as Vicki bursts into the room, tear streaks running down her face.

"Why won't you help me find this boy?" she shrieks. "My boyfriend is dead, and none of you care!"

You take a step backward behind Andi, but the movement catches Vicki's attention. "You!" Her eyes widen, and she points at you. "You killed my boyfriend!"

She begins to charge you, but one of the men holds her back. "Whoa, settle down," he says. "What are you talking about?"

"My boyfriend and I were nice enough to take this child into our home. Without warning, the brat shot my boyfriend, grabbed our food, and ran off. I was lucky to escape with my life."

Jason takes a long look at Vicki, then turns to you. "Is this true?"

To tell them about Jake and the Echo, turn to page 77.
To try to trick Vicki, turn to page 78.

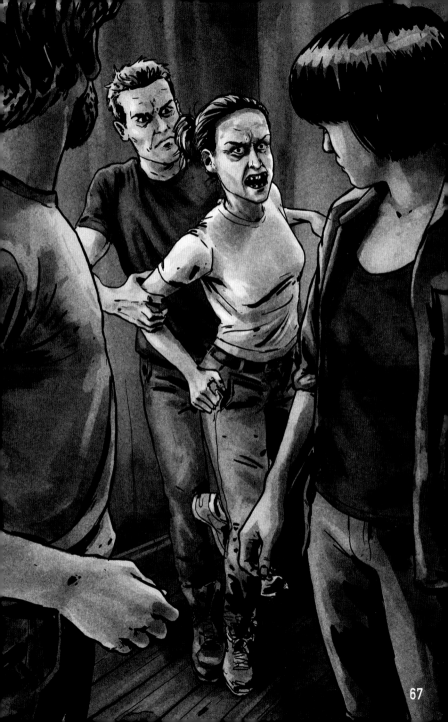

"Forget it. There's no way I can trust you," you say.

Andi gives you a sad look but nods. "I understand. For what it's worth, I really am sorry." As she turns to walk away, she adds, "There's a supermarket less than a kilometre north of here if you stay on this street. Most of the displayed food had been scavenged, but the stockroom was untouched. We've been making regular runs there for supplies. You can stock up before you go on your way."

You're touched that she would give up some of their food, but you're still fuming about being left to die. You turn on your heel without a word and head north.

Twenty minutes later you arrive at the supermarket. You step through a large window pane, doing the best you can to avoid the shattered glass. Andi was right – the shelves are bare, and the only food you see is smashed on the ground. You imagined the looting happened here around the same time as it did back home. When word spread that there wasn't a cure for the virus, rioters flooded the streets.

You look for the stockroom, which is cleverly hidden by a vending machine. With what little strength you have left, you push the machine aside and enter the stockroom.

Tinned goods line the shelves. There are cases and cases of bottled water. Several first-aid kits are within easy reach. You catch yourself with your mouth hanging open, astounded at the massive amount of supplies. But without your bag, you won't be able to take much with you.

Turn the page.

You head to the main room and walk the aisles to find something you can use to carry supplies. Your search is interrupted when you hear talking outside. You recognize the voices. It's two of the Stalkers!

"Haven't we already checked this place, Raven?" Bulldog asks.

"Yeah, we did," he replies. "But I saw someone from that survivor group leave here with all kinds of goodies. They've got to have a secret stash hidden somewhere."

The stockroom! With the vending machine out of the way, they'll easily find the supplies. You don't owe the survivor group anything, but you'd feel horrible if they lost everything because of you.

To confront the Stalkers, turn to page 71.
To try to barricade the stockroom, turn to page 76.

As Raven and Bulldog continue talking, you sneak through the aisles, away from the stockroom. The two Stalkers walk to the west side of the shop, picking through the smashed and tattered remains of the shelves. You make your way to the entrance, carefully step around the glass, and emerge outside.

"Didn't you get enough supplies when you stole my food?" you shout into the shop. Before the Stalkers can react, you turn to run, confident you can lose them in the dark. But before you can take a single step, the handle of an axe is rammed into your stomach, causing you to double over. You look up weakly at Wolf's smug face.

Raven reaches you first. "What were you doing in there, kid?"

You cough hard and wheeze as you try to catch your breath. "Just looking … for shelter," you murmur through gasps.

"I find that hard to believe," he scoffs. "So here's the deal. You can tell us where the supplies are, and we'll let you go."

"I've heard stories about you," you reply. "You *never* let someone go."

Raven lowers his head and chuckles. "Well then I suppose our reputation precedes us." He looks at his companions. "Take care of the kid."

"Not so fast!" A group of seven people runs through the car park. Each of them is carrying a gun. Bulldog reaches for his shotgun, but Andi fires first. The bullet barely misses Bulldog's feet. "Don't even think about it," she warns.

The Stalkers curse as the group makes them put down their weapons. They are forced to their knees and one of Andi's men duct tapes their hands behind their backs. Then Andi turns to you.

Turn the page.

"You saved my life, now I'm saving yours. We're even," Andi says coldly. "But you're right, there is no trust between us. Grab some supplies, then leave. I don't want to run into you again."

You nod without saying a word and go back into the supermarket. You find a laundry basket in one of the aisles. It will have to do. You head to the stockroom. After loading up with some food, water and a first-aid kit, you walk back through the shop.

The survivors are discussing what to do with the Stalkers. You want to learn their fate. But after receiving a glare from Andi, you make your way down a random street. You wonder if you'll ever find a home with other survivors.

THE END

To follow another path, turn to page 10.
To learn more about dystopias, turn to page 103.

You creep quickly but quietly back to the stockroom. There's no way you can move the machine back into place without being heard, so you enter the room and shut the door. *Just my luck – no lock*, you think. You begin to move some boxes in front of the door. The bottom breaks out of one of the boxes, and tins crash noisily to the ground.

Within seconds, one of the Stalkers pushes against the door. The boxes hold their ground temporarily but soon begin to budge. You look frantically around the room for something to defend yourself, but Bulldog crashes into the stockroom before you can act.

"Hoo-wee! Look at all dis stuff!" exclaims Bulldog.

Raven sticks his head in the room, examining the supplies. His eyes rest on you.

"We'll have our hands full carrying all this back to our place," he says. "We don't need to take the kid too."

THE END

To follow another path, turn to page 10.
To learn more about dystopias, turn to page 103.

"That is a lie!" you shout. "Her boyfriend was killed by an Echo. They kept it chained up in their living room. I just let the creature loose. If I hadn't, they would have fed me to it instead."

The room goes silent as people try to decide which one of you is telling the truth. You walk over to Andi. "Her boyfriend was the guy who attacked you," you say. "She fled after I released the Echo."

Andi gasps, drawing the attention of everyone in the room, including Jason. His grip on Vicki loosens, and she snatches a handgun from a nearby table. Jason tackles her as she fires the weapon at you, but the bullet finds its mark. Andi catches you as you fall and lays you gently on the floor. You hear someone say you're losing too much blood. Then everything goes dark.

THE END

To follow another path, turn to page 10.
To learn more about dystopias, turn to page 103.

Vicki looks like she could snap at any moment. You need to find a way to tip off Andi that Jake was the person who attacked her.

"I didn't kill your boyfriend," you say calmly. "And I didn't have anything to carry the food, so how could I steal it?"

Vicki narrows her eyes at you. "It was in a shopping trolley, you know that! You could have stashed the trolley anywhere by now."

At the mention of a shopping trolley, you see Andi's eyes widen. You exchange a quick glance, and you see her slightly roll her hands, signalling for you to keep Vicki occupied.

"If I shot your boyfriend, wouldn't I have a gun?" you ask.

"You could have put it with the shopping trolley," Vicki sneers at you. "And who's to say you don't have the gun on you now?" She looks accusingly at Jason. "Have you searched him?"

Jason looks uncomfortable. "No," he admits. He and Vicki turn to you while Jason tries to decide if he should search you. At the same time, Andi slips to the other side of the room and whispers to two of her friends. You see the movement catch Vicki's eye.

"Go ahead!" you exclaim to distract her. "Search me! You won't find anything."

As Jason steps towards you, Andi runs forward and tackles Vicki.

"WHAT ARE YOU DOING?" Vicki screams. She starts to writhe on the floor, but Andi's friends have a good hold on her.

Andi looks up at Jason and says, "Her boyfriend was the one who attacked me, and this boy saved me. This woman is lying."

Jason rests a hand on your shoulder. "Sorry to doubt you, kid," he says. Then he kneels next to Vicki and wrenches her arm behind her back. Vicki howls in pain but stops thrashing.

Turn the page.

"What do we do with her?" Jason asks.

Before anyone can respond, a shotgun blast deafens the room. You clamp your hands on your ringing ears.

"You are a rowdy bunch, ain't ya?"

Your pulse quickens at the first glance of the person speaking: It's Raven. On either side of him is Wolf and Bulldog. They each have a gun.

The shock of the new arrivals causes Jason to loosen his grip on Vicki. She jumps to her feet and backs away.

"Where do you think you're going, sweetheart?" Raven asks, raising his pistol.

"These people kidnapped me!" she says as her eyes water. "I just want to leave!"

"No one's leaving," Raven retorts. "C'mon back here."

"No! I have to get out of here!"

In all the commotion, you realize all three Stalkers have turned towards Vicki.

To try overtaking the Stalkers, turn to page 82.
To run out of the house, turn to page 83.

Andi and Jason have the same idea as you. As soon as you see Jason move, you're on your feet. Jason lowers his shoulder and throws his weight into Bulldog. Andi knocks the gun out of Raven's hand. You charge Wolf and try to grab his gun, but he kicks you backwards before you can reach him. He swings the barrel around and aims it at your head. You cringe, waiting to hear the gunshot. But before Wolf can pull the trigger, three of Andi's friends jump on him and drag him to the ground.

Jason grabs Bulldog's shotgun and levels it at Vicki. "Get over here!" he shouts as Andi ties up the Stalkers. "Tie her up too, Andi." Then he turns to you. "I'd say you've earned a good night's sleep. Second room on the left down the corridor. We'll deal with these four."

You don't argue. It seems like forever since the last time you were able to feel safe falling asleep. You're out as soon as your head hits the pillow.

THE END
To follow another path, turn to page 10.
To learn more about dystopias, turn to page 103.

You back up slowly towards the front door. Andi looks at you sternly. She mouths the word "no" and shakes her head slightly. But you're already on the move.

You flip the lock and spring out the door just as a bullet whizzes past your head. You jump off the porch and towards the gap in the fence between the two houses. Just as you are about to slip into the neighbour's yard, the cold barrel of a gun presses against the back of your head.

"Not too clever, kid," says Wolf as he throws you to the ground. "Say goodbye."

You gulp hard and try to brace yourself. But instead of hearing the blast of a gun, you feel a whoosh of air as an Echo leaps over you. The Echo pounces on Wolf. He tries to scramble away from underneath the beast, but the Echo lets out a shriek and latches onto his arm.

Turn the page.

Wolf's screams draw Bulldog to the backyard. He freezes when he sees the Echo.

"Raven! RAVEN!" he yells, backing up towards the house. He swings around at the sound of growling behind him. Two more Echoes draw close to him from opposite directions. One of the Echoes knocks him down before he can run. The other Echo turns its attention to you.

The panther-like beast crosses the yard in long strides, saliva oozing from its mouth. But just as it rears back to pounce, another Echo jumps in its path with its back to you. You recognize the scars on its back and arms. It's the Echo from Jake and Vicki's house!

The creature lets out a high-pitched wail, and the other Echo backs away. Your Echo friend nudges your shoulder and helps you stand. You walk to the front door together.

Turn the page.

Inside the house, the others have subdued Raven and Vicki. Jason's jaw drops when he sees you standing next to an Echo. One of the other survivors raises a gun at the beast.

"No!" you shout. "I saved this Echo from Vicki and her boyfriend. And it has just saved my life."

You scratch the Echo behind the ear as it lets out a forceful purr. It pushes you playfully with its head before turning and running away from the house. When it's a half a block away, it lets out an ear-splitting shriek. You jump when the Echoes from the backyard dart forward from the sides of the house and catch up with their leader.

"That's amazing," says Andi, putting an arm around you. "You've gained a powerful ally. With the Stalkers out of the picture and the Echoes at bay, we could have a chance at a peaceful life."

THE END
To follow another path, turn to page 10.
To learn more about dystopias, turn to page 103.

"Hey!" you shout as you run out of the woods, waving your hands. "Let her go!"

The man turns to you with one hand still tightly grasping the woman's hair. You immediately wish you had remained quiet when you see the size of the knife in his hand.

"You got something you wanna say to me, kid?" he sneers. "I don't take kindly to strangers."

Your heart is racing, but if you don't do something now, the woman could die. "I was just wondering why you're fighting over a few tinned goods when the house at the end of the block is loaded with supplies."

The man squints his eyes at you. "If that house is loaded, why would you bother telling me about it? Sounds like a lie to me."

You maintain eye contact with him and reply, "I've been looking for other people to help me fortify the house. Safety in numbers."

Turn the page.

The man mulls your story over. He doesn't seem convinced, so you add, "Take a look for yourself. It's the blue house on the end." You point past him down the street.

As soon as the man starts to turn his head, the woman swings her elbow into his stomach. He wheezes out a pained grunt and staggers backwards, dropping the knife. The woman pounces on the weapon and holds it in front of her, staying between the man and the shopping trolley.

"You're lucky I'm not like you!" she shouts, spitting at his feet. "Get out of here! And if I see you again, I won't be so kind!"

The man stares at the woman, uncertain what to do next. The woman takes a threatening step towards him, and he trips over his feet as he turns and hits the ground hard. He scrambles to his feet and runs between the houses and out of sight.

You walk up to the woman slowly, not wanting to catch her off guard. "Are you OK?"

She sighs deeply and turns to you. "Yeah, I'm fine. When it comes to survival, people are animals." She pauses, then adds, "Thanks, kid. Not many people would have stepped in like you did."

"I just hope that if I'm ever in that situation, someone will help me out too," you say. "The world has become a crazy place, but I'd like to think there are some genuinely good people left."

The woman smiles at you, but you're not sure if it's because she's moved by your words or if she just thinks you're naïve. "Look," she says. "I owe you one, and I'm guessing that blue house at the end of the street is as barren as the rest of them."

You don't even let her finish. "Yes! I'll come with you."

She smiles. "This way. And my name is Andi."

Turn the page.

You make small talk with Andi while walking down the street. It's clear that she knows this part of town. Although the moonlight is mainly shrouded by clouds, Andi is having no trouble navigating.

Before long, she leads you to the back door of a brick house. She softly raps the door twice, then once, then three times. A small panel in the door creaks open, and a man in his early 40s peers through at you.

"Before you say anything, Jason, I know we're not supposed to bring anyone here. But this child just saved my life."

Jason opens the door the rest of the way. "Any friend of Andi is a friend of ours," he says, shaking your hand firmly as you enter the house. "Besides, we could use another able body. Some of us were just going to head out for supplies. You can come and help us if you're up for it."

To stay at the house and rest, turn to page 92.
To go with Jason for supplies, turn to page 94.

"I would love to help, but I am absolutely exhausted," you say. "I've been on the move most of the day after Stalkers stole all my food."

As soon as you say "Stalkers," the smile drops from Jason's face. He and Andi exchange an anxious look. Several people from the other room move into the doorway and stare at you intently.

"Take the rest of the group with you," Andi says quietly to Jason. "And make sure everyone has a gun." Jason breathes deeply and nods. He turns to talk to the others that have gathered near by. After a couple of moments, they each grab a gun and head out of the door.

"We had a nasty run-in with the Stalkers a few weeks ago," says Andi. "We've had to stay on the move, which is why it made sense to keep our supplies offsite. But I think the Stalkers are closing in on us again."

Andi leads you to a bedroom and sits down on the bed next to you.

"Get some sleep, kid," she says. "And thanks again for coming to my rescue."

SKREEEEEEEE!

Your breath catches in your throat. Andi's eyes go wide with fear.

SKREEEEEEEE!

You snap your head around. Andi squeezes your hand. The shriek is closer, but it came from the other side of the house.

"It's an Echo," whispers Andi.

"What's that?" you whisper back.

"Bloodthirsty panther-like creatures. No one knows where they came fr—"

A loud crash on the other side of the house interrupts Andi's sentence. A low growl travels down the corridor.

To run for a gun, turn to page 99.
To hide under the bed, turn to page 100.

"I'm up for it. Just tell me what to do."

"Great! A nearby supermarket has a fully supplied stockroom. We propped a vending machine in front of the door so no one else would find it. Keep your eyes peeled for Echoes." Before you can ask what Echoes are, the group is off. Moving at a fast pace, you're out of breath when you reach the supermarket.

"Okay, Curt, Hanne and Andrew will load up while you and I stand guard," says Jason. "Make it quick!" They crouch through a shattered window and into the shop. You remain quiet and keep your eyes peeled.

"Look what we have here."

Silhouettes emerge from behind a car. The Stalkers! Raven keeps a gun focused on Jason. Wolf grabs your arm and pulls it behind your back. The pain causes you to fall to your knees.

"What are you doing out so late at night?" asks Raven with a grin.

To stay quiet, turn to page 96.
To tell them about the stockroom, turn to page 97.

You exchange a glance with Jason, but neither of you says a word.

"Look," says Raven. "You're obviously part of a bigger group, and we want to know where you're staying."

"No," says Jason immediately. "There's no way I'm giving up the rest of my group."

"I see," responds Raven. "Well, you have a choice. Give up the location of your group, or your friend dies."

"Are you kidding? You'll kill us either way," Jason says.

"You said it," says Raven. He saunters over to you and removes the pistol from his waistband. Jason screams at Raven as he hunches down to your eye level. Without hesitation, he brings his arm back and swings the pistol around, hitting you squarely in the head.

Maybe Raven was bluffing to get information, you think before blacking out. But the Stalkers' reputation doesn't give you much hope that you'll ever wake up.

THE END

To follow another path, turn to page 10.
To learn more about dystopias, turn to page 103.

"We just showed up to get food and supplies," you say quickly. "If you let us live, we'll show you where we're hiding the goods."

Jason glares at you angrily as Raven chuckles. "We've searched this place before and haven't found anything," he scoffs. "But by all means, lead the way."

Wolf jabs a gun into your back, and you march through the broken window with Raven, Bulldog and Jason close behind. As you near the middle of the shop, you purposely slip on a smashed bag of crisps. You hit the ground hard and let out a painful yell.

"Will you watch where your goin'!" says Bulldog. "On your feet!"

You use the empty shelf to haul yourself up and continue towards the stockroom.

Turn the page.

You feel a stab of dread when you see the vending machine pushed aside, exposing the stockroom. You hope your yell gave the others enough time to hide.

"In there," you say, pointing to the stockroom door.

"Bulldog, check it out," commands Raven.

Bulldog kicks in the stockroom door with his shotgun raised. The gun falls to his side when he sees the massive amount of food, water and supplies.

"Raven, we hit the jackpot!" he squeals happily.

"Too bad you won't get any of it," says Curt as he points his gun at Raven. Hanne disarms Wolf, and Andrew walks towards Bulldog, aiming down the sight of his gun. Bulldog drops his weapon disgustedly.

"Thanks for the heads up, kid," says Ramon. "You gave us enough time to flank you guys. Jason, I think we have a valuable addition to our group." You smile as Jason nods in agreement.

THE END
To follow another path, turn to page 10.
To learn more about dystopias, turn to page 103.

If the creature is the size of a panther, you'll need a weapon. But the moment you step into the corridor, the creature's head emerges from around the corner.

Andi pulls you into the bedroom and slams the door. She moves the bed in front of the door, and just in time. You hear the Echo's claws clicking on the hardwood floor as it walks down the corridor.

Suddenly, gunfire erupts outside. The Echo's loud footsteps shake the floor as it runs from the house. Then there's a knock on the door. It's Jason!

"We saw the Echo approach the house after we left," says Jason. "They're getting more aggressive. I hate to say it, but we have to leave town."

That morning, the group packs up its belongings. You stop at the supermarket and load up with supplies. Although you're on the road again, the security of being with other people leaves you feeling optimistic about the future.

THE END
To follow another path, turn to page 10.
To learn more about dystopias, turn to page 103.

You motion for Andi to go under the bed. As soon as she does, you slide next to her and try to steady your breathing. Andi grips your hand tightly when you hear sharp clicking approaching the bedroom.

With a crash, the bedroom door flies off its hinges and slams forcefully onto the bed. You can't help but whimper when you see the Echo's scaly black feet. The creature's claws click loudly against the floor. Its head comes into view as it sniffs intensely near the bed. Then it lets out a piercing shriek.

You instinctively cover your ears as they ring painfully. That small movement grabs the Echo's attention. It catches the sleeve of your shirt and drags you from your hiding place You try to roll away, but it steps on your chest with a heavy paw. You see Andi dash out from under the bed. You can only hope she makes it out alive.

THE END

To follow another path, turn to page 10.
To learn more about dystopias, turn to page 103.

LIVING IN A BLEAK WORLD

A worldwide virus outbreak. A flesh-eating zombie horde. A devastating nuclear winter. All of these scenarios – and many more – could lead to a dystopian future. While the details of each dystopia will differ, many of the events leading up to it will be similar.

It all starts with rumours. News stories describe an incurable disease or an asteroid on course to collide with Earth. Other outlets pick up on it, and word will spread quickly through social media. Unless the rumours are laid to rest, panic sets in.

Once people abandon their day-to-day lives, the order of society may begin to fall apart. People may start to loot, especially if there is a short supply of important items such as food, water or medication. Angry mobs may erupt in violence in the streets.

Before long, the government – and society, in general – will begin to crumble. In many apocalyptic stories, this can be even scarier than the actual doomsday event. People who are scared and trying to survive may act out of character. Some people may panic. Most will usually hunker down and try to wait out the chaos.

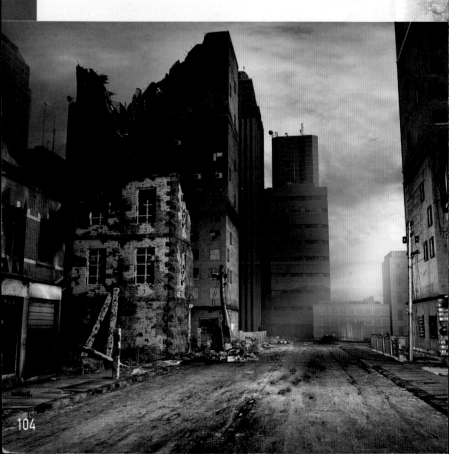

Then the event that started the panic occurs. Depending on the event, a majority of the world's population won't survive. Those that remain will have to cope with the loss of their loved ones while trying to find shelter, supplies and other survivors.

Although a dystopian future can be scary to think about, we can sleep a little easier knowing that the government is one step ahead. From pandemics to global natural disasters and even zombie outbreaks, government organizations such as the World Health Organization (WHO) and the Health Protection Agency have emergency plans in place.

Just like a family plans an escape route from their house in case of a fire, these organizations have mapped out several steps in case of a doomsday event. Some steps are taken in advance to prevent the event from occurring. Others are used to limit the amount of human casualties. Knowing that there are doomsday plans already in place can help avoid widespread panic and chaos.

DYSTOPIAN SURVIVAL

How do you plan for an event that could happen in so many different ways? It's really not any different than planning for any other disaster. Regardless of the event that led to the dystopia, there are some basic supplies you'll need to help you survive.

SURVIVAL KIT

*Water
*Non-perishable food and a can opener
*A first-aid kit and any medication you may need
*A torch and batteries
*A variety of clothes (for all types of weather)
*Blankets
*Lighter
*Tools or supplies that have many uses, such as a Swiss army knife and duct tape

Other items that are helpful in a disaster, such as mobile phones, televisions and radios, might not be useful in a dystopia. In this book's scenario, most of the world's population has been wiped out, so electronic communication probably wouldn't be possible.

Tailor your survival pack for your specific situation. Food and water are the most important in any survival situation. Remember, if you're on the move, it's important to take only what you need. If your lighter runs out of fluid or you can't find any more torch batteries, it might be better to leave them behind.

TEN TIPS ON HOW TO SURVIVE IN A DYSTOPIA

- **Trust is hard to earn.** Not only should you be on your guard when you meet strangers, remember that other people will have the same guarded approach when they meet you.

- **Stock up in advance.** When news hits that the world is coming to an end, there will probably be looting and rioting in the streets. You'll need to have all your supplies before things get nasty.

- **Shelter is important, so choose it wisely.** If you had to leave your home during the catastrophic event that led to the dystopia, find a building in a non-populated area that has many exits.

- **Going solo can be incredibly hard**. If you can find a group of people you can trust, there is definitely safety in numbers.

- **Food may be scarce**. Plan out your daily rations in advance so you don't run out.

- **Big cities are better to avoid at the beginning**. But if the government sets up a camp to help survivors, it will probably be in a major city.

- **Be wary of water**. Drinking water may be scarce, but unless you find it in an unopened bottle, don't guzzle it down. It could be contaminated. Boil the water before drinking it. The high temperature helps sterilize the water.

- **Keep your survival kit near by**. You may need to run at any moment, and you don't want to leave your basic supplies behind. Keep a couple of days' worth of food and water with you at all times.

- **Travel during the day**. You might not know all the dangers that await you in a dystopia, so it's better to face them in the light.

- **If possible, move somewhere that has warm weather all year round**. It will be easier to survive if you don't have to battle a harsh winter or blazing hot summers.

GLOSSARY

ACUTE sharp or severe

AMBUSH surprise attack

ANTIDOTE something that has a countering effect to a
poison or disease

BARRICADE block a person's access by using a wall or
other type of barrier to cause a separation

CAPTOR person who is imprisoning another person

CONTAMINATED unfit for use because of contact with a
harmful substance

DEHYDRATION life-threatening medical condition caused
by a lack of water

DISCREET choosing the right thing to say

DYSTOPIA dangerous and bleak world most likely to have
been created by a catastrophic event such as a virus
outbreak or nuclear war

EXHAUSTION state of extreme mental or physical fatigue

HYBRID plant or animal that has been bred from two
different species or varieties

INCURABLE describes diseases that cannot be cured

INFILTRATE join an enemy's side secretly to gain information or cause damage

PANDEMIC disease that spreads over a wide area and affects many people

PRECEDE come before something

SCARCE hard to find

SCAVENGE search for food and supplies

STERILIZE clean something thoroughly so that no germs or dirt remain

WELD join two pieces of metal together until they melt

READ MORE

Can You Survive The Wilderness? (You Choose: Survival), Matt Doeden (Raintree, 2014)

Nuclear Disaster (A World After), Alex Woolf (Raintree, 2014)

Surviving Disasters (Extreme Survival), Nick Hunter (Raintree 2012)

The Soterion Mission, Stewart Ross (Curious Fox, 2013)

WEBSITE

www.rwjf.org/en/culture-of-health/2013/12/the_five_deadliesto.html

Learn about the five deadliest outbreaks and pandemics in history.

AUTHOR

Anthony Wacholtz is a writer and editor with a love of things that go bump in the night. He lives with his wife, Katrina, and dog, Max, in Minnesota, USA where he is ready and waiting for the zombie apocalypse.

ILLUSTRATOR

James Nathan attended Worcester College of Art and Design in England and received a degree in Illustration at Cardiff School of Art and Design. His artwork is mainly fantasy and science fiction based, inspired by Pixar illustrations as well as the artist Dan LuVisi. James lives in Bristol, with his girlfriend and cat. In his spare time he enjoys making music, as well as music videos.